steve, Terror of the seas

Steve, Terror of the seas

megan Brewis

OXFORD

UNIVERSITY PRESS

Hi, I'm Steve.

I'm a VERY scary fish.

Small fish are scared of me.

And **BIG** fish are scared of me.

Even fish who are not fish
are scared of me.

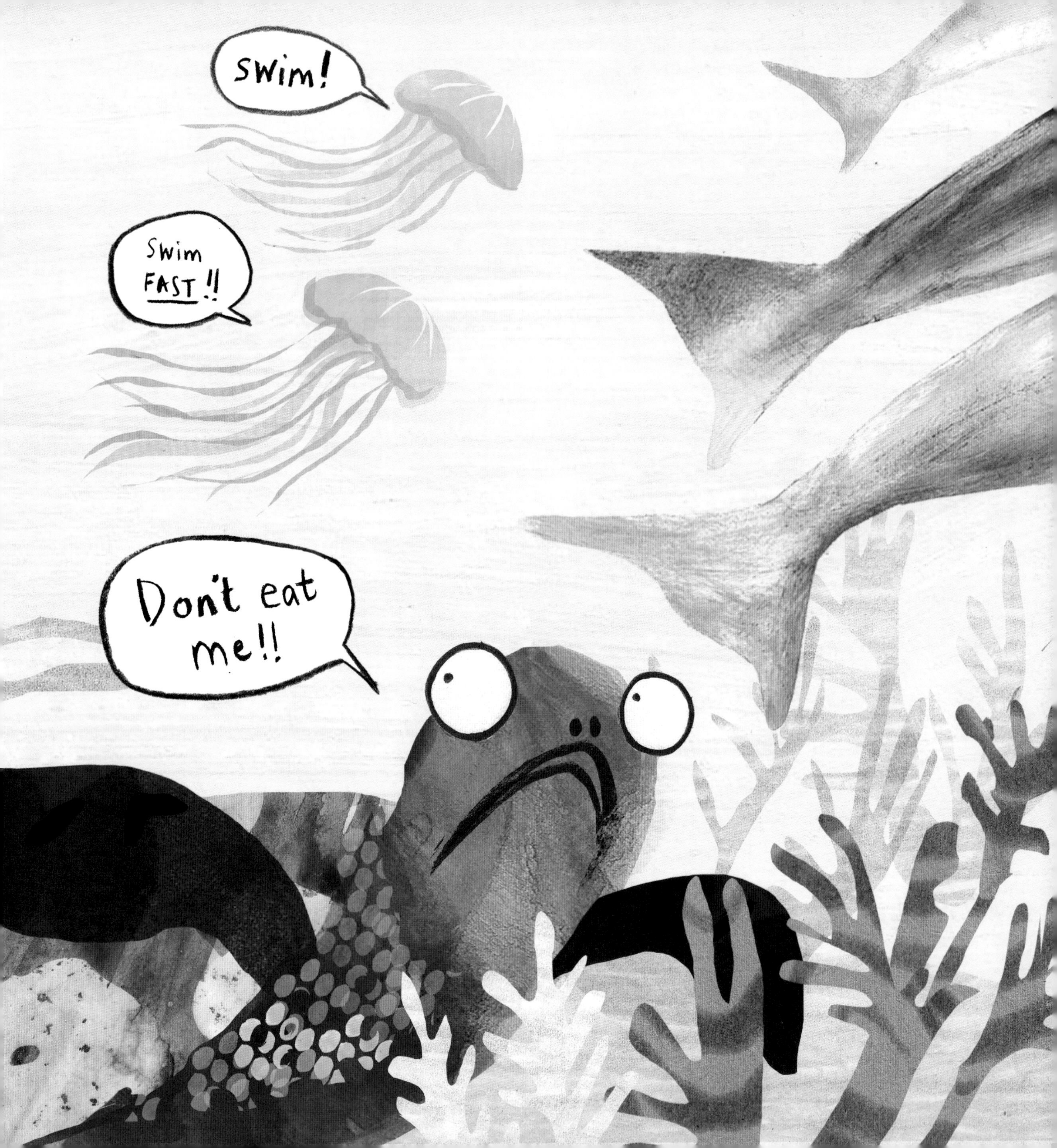
SWIM!
Swim FAST!!
Don't eat me!!

EVERYONE under the sea is afraid.

And as for humans . . .

...they are terrified!

I'm not sure what it is that
makes me so scary . . .

I'm not particularly big.

About 30 cm

My teeth aren't too bad . . .

. . . are they?

And though I'm no angelfish . . .

I've seen far *scarier* fish in these waters.
Have a look for yourself . . .

My own personal favourite is
the **TOAD FISH.**
It actually croaks!

Not sure why
I'm even on
this page...

And let's not forget
the **BLOB FISH.**

Blob.

Finding love has been a challenge.

And being scary
can seem like a lonely life.

But you haven't met my best friend, George . . .

We go EVERYWHERE together.

Hey George!

And George doesn't think I'm scary at all!

THE TRUE PART

The ocean can be a dangerous place for fish, as there are many hungry predators around!

Some fish swim in large groups, called schools, or shoals.

This gives them the appearance of being larger than they really are, and protects them from bigger fish.

Steve is a Pilot fish.

Pilot fish choose a very big, scary friend to protect them!

In return for keeping them safe,
Pilot fish keep sharks free of harmful parasites.

This friendship is called a mutualistic relationship.
Sharks even allow Pilot fish to clean their teeth!

(Pilot fish are not really scary at all !!)

Smile, George! Show them your shiny teeth!

For Jackson—M.B.

OXFORD
UNIVERSITY PRESS

Great Clarendon Street, Oxford OX2 6DP

Oxford University Press is a department of the University of Oxford.
It furthers the University's objective of excellence in research, scholarship,
and education by publishing worldwide.

Oxford is a registered trade mark of Oxford University Press
in the UK and in certain other countries

Text and illustrations copyright © Megan Brewis 2018

First published in 2018

British Library Cataloguing in Publication Data
Data available

ISBN: 978-0-19-276685-4 (paperback)

10 9 8 7 6 5 4 3 2 1

Printed in China

Paper used in the production of this book is a natural,
recyclableproduct made from wood grown in sustainable forests.
The manufacturing process conforms to the environmental
regulations of the country of origin.